THE BIG CHANCE

JOHN COLDWELL

Illustrated by Sonia Hollyman

OXFORD
UNIVERSITY PRESS

Great Clarendon Street, Oxford OX2 6DP

Oxford University Press is a department of the University of Oxford.
It furthers the University's objective of excellence in research, scholarship,
and education by publishing worldwide in

Oxford New York
Auckland Cape Town Dar es Salaam Hong Kong Karachi
Kuala Lumpur Madrid Melbourne Mexico City Nairobi
New Delhi Shanghai Taipei Toronto

With offices in
Argentina Austria Brazil Chile Czech Republic France Greece
Guatemala Hungary Italy Japan Poland Portugal Singapore
South Korea Switzerland Thailand Turkey Ukraine Vietnam

First published 1996
This edition 2005

British Library Cataloguing in Publication Data
Data available

ISBN-13: 978-0-19-917984-8
ISBN-10: 0-19-917984-0

3 5 7 9 10 8 6 4 2

Available in packs
Stage 11 More Stories A Pack of 6:
ISBN-13: 978-0-19-917983-1; ISBN-10: 0-19-917983-2
Stage 11 More Stories A Class Pack:
ISBN-13: 978-0-19-917990-9; ISBN-10: 0-19-917990-5
Guided Reading Cards also available:
ISBN-13: 978-0-19-917992-3; ISBN-10: 0-19-917992-1

Cover artwork by Sonia Holleyman
Photograph of John Coldwell © Caroline Scott Photography, Staplehurst

Printed in China by Imago

'Drink your tea'

Ray Martin, the new boss of Smalltown Football Club, was very happy. It was almost half-time and his team were winning 1–0.

Ray raced down to the changing room to talk to the team. Eleven cups of tea were waiting for the players.

The team jogged in, looking tired but happy.

'Well done, lads,' smiled Ray. 'You must be thirsty. Drink your tea while it's hot.'

'In a minute, boss,' said Steve the captain.

Then Ray noticed one player after another taking their cups of tea into the shower room. When they came back the cups were empty.

'That's funny,' thought Ray. 'Drinking tea in the shower.'

Steve the captain picked up his cup. Ray followed him. In the shower room Steve was pouring his tea down the sink.

'What's going on?' said Ray.

Steve leaped in the air and dropped his cup. The sound of the smashing cup brought the other players running.

'It was his fault,' sobbed Steve. 'He made me jump.'

'What shall we do?' moaned Nick the goalkeeper.

'Maybe we can glue it,' said Steve.

'Will somebody tell me what's going on?' said Ray. 'Why are you all tipping your tea down the sink?'

Nobody spoke.

'Well?'

'Because it's not very nice.'

'Why all the fuss about a broken cup?'

'Hilda,' whispered somebody.

'Who is this Hilda?'

'She makes the tea,' hissed Nick.

'Then I shall go and tell her that the tea is not very nice.'

'Ssh,' hissed the team. 'She'll hear you.'

'She certainly will hear me,' said Ray.

'Oh dear,' said Nick.

'Fancy,' said Ray. 'A bunch of men, scared of a little old tea lady.'

'Er,' said one player. 'She's not little.'

'She's not that old,' said another.

'And we're not scared of her,' said Steve. 'We're terrified.'

'That's enough,' said Ray. 'Where will I find this Hilda?'

'At the tea stand,' said Nick.

Ray strode towards the door.

'Good luck,' said someone.

Ray meets Hilda

The tea stand was an old caravan. Ray joined a quiet queue of fans.

'I'd like one cup of tea please, with a dash of milk and no sugar,' said a big man.

'You'll get it how I make it and you'll like it,' boomed a voice from inside the caravan.

The next man in the queue already had a cup of tea. 'Excuse me,' he said politely.

'Yes,' boomed the voice.

'I'm sorry to bother you,' continued the man. 'But this tea is not very nice.'

'What did you say?'

The caravan began to tremble. The caravan rocked and shook. There was a great bang and the door flew off its hinges.

There in the hole where the door had been stood Hilda. She wore a green skirt, an apron, red boots and a jumper that said, 'Smalltown F.C.'

'Hilda,' gasped Ray.

Hilda stepped down from the caravan, rolling up her sleeves.

She strode over to the man.

'Do you know what I do with great moaning minnies who come complaining about my tea?'

'I-I don't know,' stammered the man.

'I do this,' said Hilda.

Hilda grabbed the man and threw him over her shoulder. She marched down towards the pitch.

'Help!' cried the man.

Hilda strode into the goal area.

She lifted the man over her head and sat him on the cross bar.

'Get me down,' yelled the man.

Hilda marched back to her tea stand.

'What are you looking at?' she said to one supporter.

'Nothing.'

'Is that cup on the floor yours?'

'I-er.'

'Put it in the bin.'

Hilda climbed back into the caravan.

'Right,' said Hilda. 'Any more complaints?'

'I think I'll talk to Hilda after the game,' said Ray to himself.

A group of fans helped the man down from the goalpost.

'Excuse me,' Ray asked them. 'But if the tea is so horrible, why do you buy it?'

One of the fans looked up towards the tea stand. 'It's OK,' he said. 'She's looking the other way.'

'If you don't buy a cup of tea,' whispered another, 'she comes out and makes you drink two cups.'

'So,' said another, 'it's safer to buy a cup and tip it away.'

Ray looked around. All over the terraces were puddles of tea.

'She'll have to go,' said Ray to himself.

Ray walked back to the changing room. The players had just left to start the second half. Instead of watching the game, Ray paced up and down.

The game ended in a 3–1 win for Smalltown F.C. As the players trotted into the changing room, Ray patted them on the back.

'Right,' he said bravely. 'I'm off to see Hilda.'

The players crowded into the shower room. Nick, the goalkeeper, climbed up on Steve's shoulders. He looked out of the window.

'What's going on?' asked the others.

'He's reached the tea stand.'

'Yes.'

'He's talking to Hilda. Oh no! He's on his way back.'

The players raced out of the shower room, leaving Nick hanging onto the window ledge.

'Oi, lads,' yelled Nick. 'Get me down!'

The changing room door opened. In staggered Ray, with a tea urn rammed on his head.

'You told her, then,' said Steve, as he pulled the urn off.

The changing room door flew open and Hilda marched in. 'Where do you think you are going with my tea urn?'

Just then there was a terrific crash from the shower room.

Everybody raced into the shower room.

Nick was lying on the floor.

'I fell,' he moaned. 'My leg really hurts.'

'He won't be able to play next week,' said Steve sadly.

'That's the cup game against City,' said Hilda.

'That is all I need,' groaned Ray. 'A goalkeeper who can't make saves and a tea lady who can't make tea.'

'What did you say?' roared Hilda.

The changing room fell silent.

'I...' began Ray.

Suddenly, Hilda gave a great sob.

'Do you think I don't know what goes on?' she sighed. 'I've seen people tipping their tea away. I've tried so hard to make a nice cup of tea. But I just can't. It always goes wrong.'

Then Hilda pulled her apron over her head and cried. The players had never seen Hilda cry. It was more frightening than any of her tempers.

Ray put his arm around Hilda's shoulder.

'I'm sorry,' he said. 'I should never have said anything about your tea.'

'But it's true,' wailed Hilda.

'What can I do to make it up to you?' asked Ray.

Hilda slowly let the apron fall. A little smile crept across her face. 'You could let me play in goal on Saturday.'

'Impossible,' said Ray.

'But there's no one else,' said Steve.

'I'll think about it,' said Ray.

'Think about it,' sniffed Hilda. 'If I don't play on Saturday, two things will happen. One. We will lose against City because we haven't got a goalkeeper.'

'And the other?'

'I shall stuff you back in that tea urn for not letting me play.'

'Gentlemen,' said Ray. 'May I introduce Hilda, our new goalie.'

A proper goalkeeper

The two teams raced onto the pitch to a great roar from the crowd. Hilda strode towards the goal at the City fans' end.

Someone in the crowd yelled, 'That's not a proper goalkeeper. It's the tea lady!'

Slowly Hilda turned.

'Who said that?' she growled.

The crowd fell silent.

'I asked who spoke?'

She pointed into the crowd.

'It was you. Come here.'

Nervously, a man wearing a long City scarf came to the front of the crowd.

'Right, you squirt,' snarled Hilda. 'You sit here, by the goal, where I can keep an eye on you. As for the rest of you City fans, you may cheer your team, but no rude comments about me. Got it?'

'Yes, Hilda,' chanted the City fans.

The game began. Almost at once, City were on the attack. The centre forward broke through and rushed towards the goal. He was about to shoot when he saw Hilda running at him.

'Yaar!' screamed Hilda.

The player was so shocked that he kicked the ball over the bar and into the crowd. The City fans groaned.

'Ball, please,' snapped Hilda.

Hilda booted the ball up the pitch.

By half-time neither team had scored.

'Well played, everybody,' smiled Ray. As he went round talking to the players, he noticed something odd.

Everyone was happily drinking their tea.

The second half dragged and nobody looked like scoring.

Hilda looked at her watch. It was nearly time. She turned to the fans behind her.

'What happens if it's a draw?' she asked.

'You have to play half an hour's extra time,' shouted someone.

'Another half an hour of standing around in the cold?' said Hilda. 'Blow that.'

She marched up the pitch. A City player had the ball. Hilda charged towards him. He was so surprised that he passed the ball to Hilda instead of his own team.

Hilda steamed up the pitch, yelling, 'I want this game finished. Out of my way.'

And that is what all the players did. Hilda scored.

The referee blew the final whistle and the Smalltown team carried Hilda round on their shoulders. They let her collect the cup.

'If you all love Hilda, clap your hands,' chanted someone in the crowd. The ground shook with the sound of the fans clapping.

'Listen to that,' shouted Steve. 'They love you.'

'You're right,' sniffed Hilda. 'They do. Now let's fill this cup with tea.'

'Hang on,' cried Nick. He limped onto the pitch pushing a trolley. There was a slightly dented urn on the trolley. He poured the tea into the cup. All the players took a great gulp of delicious tea.

'So it was you who made the tea,' said Steve.

The simple end to this story would be that Nick went on making the tea and Hilda played in goal. But as soon as Nick's leg was better he told Ray that he wanted to play again.

'That's great,' said Ray.

'What about Hilda?' said Nick.

'Leave that to me,' said Ray with a smile.

Hilda was trying to fix the door back on the caravan.

'Can you stop for a minute?' said Ray.

Hilda put down her tools.

'I'd like to thank you for playing in goal,' he began.

'But Nick's leg is better and you don't want me in goal any more,' said Hilda.

'How did you know what I was going to say?'

'I'm not daft,' said Hilda, dabbing her eyes with a hankie.

'There's something else,' said Ray. 'I want the club to look more modern. So I'm getting rid of this old caravan.'

'Oh,' sniffed Hilda. 'So you don't want me at all.'

'Yes, I do,' smiled Ray. 'So do all the fans and the team. That's why I am going to put you in charge of a brand new automatic tea machine.'